DATE DUE			
JA 30 '92	JY 8 '9	OCT 12 93	MY 24 '07
FE 11 '9	AG 2 '9	NOV 29 93	MY 06 '0
MR 21 '9	OC 1 93	JAN 11	JE 2 '01
AP 13 '9	OC 16 93	APR 02 '07	MY 31 '8
MY 20 '92	OC 29 93	MAY 14	
JY 2 '92	DEC 93	OCT 14	AG 7 6 '9
JY 30 '9	DEC 23 93	JA 22 02	
OC 6 '9	SEP 08 '94	AG 08 01	
NO 27 '9	SEP 26 '94	SE 11 02	
FE 17 '9	JAN 06	MY 13 '05	
AP 29 '93	JUL 0	AG 19 '05	
JE 30 '9	AUG 14	AP 04 07	

201-9500   PRINTED IN U.S.A.

E
Raz   Razzi, Jim
           Alice's Wonderland
           adventure

WALT DISNEY®

CHOOSE YOUR OWN ADVENTURE®

ALICE'S WONDERLAND ADVENTURE

Story adapted by JIM RAZZI

77728

Bantam 🐓 **Books**

TORONTO • NEW YORK • LONDON • SYDNEY • AUCKLAND

RL 2, 004–008

ALICE'S WONDERLAND ADVENTURE

A Bantam Book / October 1985

CHOOSE YOUR OWN ADVENTURE® is a registered trademark of Bantam Books, Inc. Registered in U.S. Patent and Trademark Office and elsewhere.

Concept: Edward Packard; Series Development: R.A. Montgomery and Edward Packard.

Library of Congress Cataloging in Publication Data

Razzi, Jim.
 Alice's Wonderland adventure.

 (Walt Disney choose your own adventure)
 Summary: The reader joins Alice for some adventures in Wonderland, the outcomes of which are self-determining.
  1. Children's stories, American. 2. Plot-your-own stories. [1. Fantasy. 2. Plot-your-own stories]
I. Carroll, Lewis, 1832–1898. Alice's adventures in Wonderland. II. Title. III. Series.
PZ7.R233Al 1985   [E]   85-7361
ISBN 0-553-05405-8

Published simultaneously in the United States and Canada

Bantam Books are published by Bantam Books, Inc. Its trademark, consisting of the words "Bantam Books" and the portrayal of a rooster, is Registered in U.S. Patent and Trademark Office and in other countries. Marca Registrada. Bantam Books, Inc., 666 Fifth Avenue, New York, New York 10103.

PRINTED IN THE UNITED STATES OF AMERICA

DW   0 9 8 7 6 5 4 3 2 1

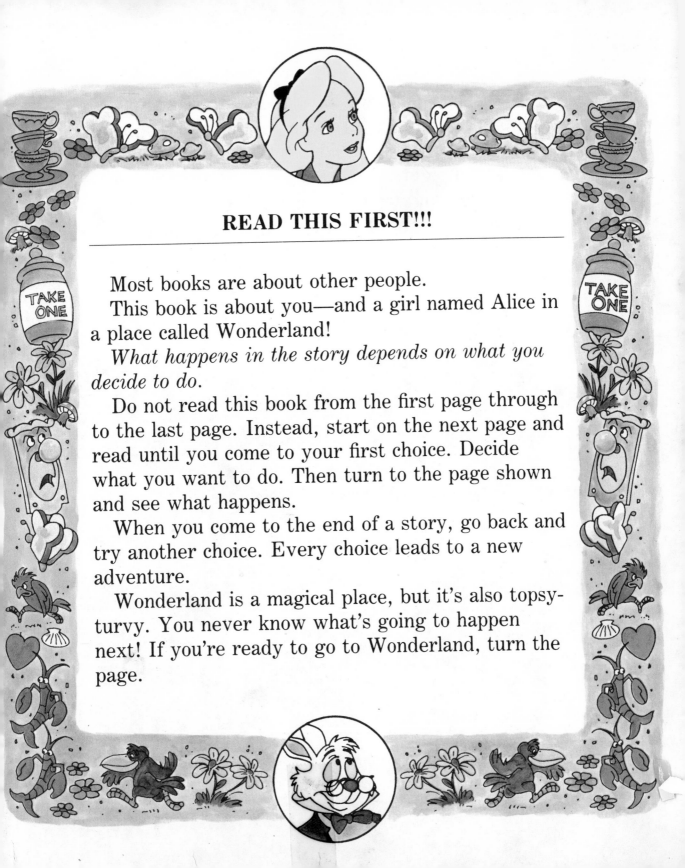

READ THIS FIRST!!!

Most books are about other people.

This book is about you—and a girl named Alice in a place called Wonderland!

What happens in the story depends on what you decide to do.

Do not read this book from the first page through to the last page. Instead, start on the next page and read until you come to your first choice. Decide what you want to do. Then turn to the page shown and see what happens.

When you come to the end of a story, go back and try another choice. Every choice leads to a new adventure.

Wonderland is a magical place, but it's also topsy-turvy. You never know what's going to happen next! If you're ready to go to Wonderland, turn the page.

It is a lazy summer day, and you are sitting by the bank of a peaceful river, enjoying the sunshine.

A swan gracefully glides by, and you watch until it is out of sight.

You sigh and lean back against a tree. You are feeling happy and drowsy. You close your eyes. . . .

Go on to the next page.

You are just dozing off when you hear someone shout, "Wait!"

You open your eyes and see a girl running by. She looks as if she's chasing someone.

You jump up and run alongside her.

"Where are you going?" you ask.

The girl looks at you in surprise.

"I haven't got time to talk," she says. "I might lose him!"

Turn to page 2.

"Lose who?" you ask. "Who are you chasing?"

"The White Rabbit!" answers the girl.

You are about to ask her why she is chasing a white rabbit when she cries, "Look! He's going in that hole!"

And without another word, the girl crawls into a hole nearby. You don't know what's going on, but you want to find out.

"Wait for me!" you shout.

Go on to the next page.

You crawl into the hole, too—and find yourself falling through space! But you are falling in slow motion.

Presently you notice that you are floating past cupboards and shelves, clocks and mirrors. Maybe you could grab for something and break your fall. Or you could let yourself continue to float downward.

If you make a grab for something, turn to page 4.

If you let yourself continue to fall, turn to page 6.

You grab for a cupboard and scramble inside. But you are surprised to find that the inside of the cupboard is a long tunnel spiraling downward.

You try to crawl back out, but the sides are too steep. You slide down at breakneck speed!

Suddenly you shoot out the end—and land right on top of someone!

Turn to page 7.

You float down and down until you land with a thump at the bottom of the hole. You look around for the girl, but she's nowhere in sight. In front of you is a passage with doors all along it. You run to the end and reach another passageway. This one is flooded.

"Now, where did she go?" you say aloud.

"Through my keyhole, into my garden!" says a doorknob.

Turn to page 10.

You don't know *who* is underneath you, but you look up and recognize the girl you followed down the rabbit hole. And suddenly you realize that you and the girl are surrounded by giant playing cards!

You must have gotten smaller! What's going on? Is it magic, you wonder?

The girl looks at you. "Oh, dear!" she says. "I'm afraid you just fell on the Queen of Hearts! Let's run before she gets mad and has our heads!"

Turn to page 8.

8   You dash after the girl. "What's your name?" you ask.

"Alice," she replies.

"I'm very glad to meet you," you say.

"I'm glad to meet you, too!"

You and Alice run through a dark forest until you come to a fork in the road.

Go on to the next page.

"Which way should we go?" says Alice.

Suddenly you notice two signs on a tree. One says THIS WAY, and the other says THAT WAY.

"Well?" asks Alice.

You shrug and say, "We can either go THIS WAY or THAT WAY, I think we should go . . .

If you say THIS WAY, turn to page 24.

If you say THAT WAY, turn to page 12.

You jump with surprise. A talking doorknob!

But you recover quickly and say, "How can I get into your garden?"

"Just wish you were there!" says the doorknob. "I find it's much simpler that way."

You can't believe it will be that easy, but you close your eyes and wish, anyway.

When you open them again, you find yourself in a beautiful garden.

"It worked!" you cry.

Go on to the next page.

Just then you see the girl again. You have both
shrunk to the size of the flowers in the garden.

"Hello," you say. "What's your name?"

"Alice," answers the girl.

At that very moment the White Rabbit runs by—
and he's all dressed up! You ask Alice what she
wants to do—follow the rabbit or forget him and go
exploring.

"What do *you* think we should do?" she asks.

---

*If you decide to follow the White Rabbit,
turn to page 14.*

*If you decide that you and Alice should go
exploring, turn to page 18.*

You and Alice follow the path to THAT WAY.

You have gone only a little way when you see a Cheshire Cat on the branch of a tree.

"Excuse me, Cheshire Puss," you say, "are we going the right way for THAT WAY?"

Instead of answering, the Cheshire Cat just grins.

Go on to the next page.

"Excuse me," you say again, "but we would like to know where THAT WAY leads to." 13

The cat just keeps grinning from ear to ear.

"Excuse me, too," says Alice timidly, "but why are you grinning?"

"Why are you asking so many questions?" asks the cat, pointing to Alice.

"Because we want to know where THAT WAY leads to!" you say a bit angrily.

Turn to page 30.

14   You and Alice chase after the White Rabbit. He runs down a path and into a small house, all the while saying, "Oh, my fur and whiskers, I'm late! I'm late!"

You are just about to follow the White Rabbit into the house when he dashes out again.

"Don't just stand there," he calls to Alice. "Go inside and fetch my gloves!"

Go on to the next page.

Alice is so surprised that she runs into the house
to do as the White Rabbit asks.

"Wait for me!" you yell.

You and Alice look everywhere, but you can't find
the White Rabbit's gloves.

"I don't think we're going to find them at all,"
says Alice.

You can't find the gloves, but you do find a cookie
jar labeled TAKE ONE.

Go on to the next page.

The cover is on tightly, however, and you will have to work to get it off.

From outside you hear the White Rabbit call, "Hurry, please. Seconds count. The Queen will be very angry if I'm late!"

Go on to the next page.

You don't want the White Rabbit to get into trouble, but as Alice said, you probably won't ever find his gloves. And you *are* hungry. Should you stop to eat some cookies, or should you keep looking for the gloves?

If you eat some cookies, turn to page 22.

If you keep looking for the gloves, turn to page 28.

18   The White Rabbit scampers away, and you and
Alice turn and run in the opposite direction.
Soon you come to another garden.
"What kind of flowers are *you*?" asks a flower.
"We're not flowers," says Alice as a bread-and-
butterfly glides by. She doesn't seem at all surprised
to hear the flower speak.
"Then you must be weeds!" says a daisy. "Be off
with you!"

Go on to the next page.

Talking flowers! Bread-and-butterflies! You've never seen anything like this in your life!

But the flowers aren't very friendly, so you and Alice leave the garden and run down a tangled path.

Turn to page 20.

The path leads to a small beach, where a strange race is going on. It has no beginning and no end— everyone just runs around and around a rock.

"Would you hold this?" asks Alice, as she hands you a little golden key. "I want to join the race."

You hold the key in your hand and watch the runners. But the race is making you dizzy. You close your eyes for a moment . . .

Go on to the next page.

. . . and when you open them, you're back on the riverbank. Was it all a dream?

You feel something in your hand. You are still holding the key that Alice gave you!

You wonder if you can find your way back to the long hall at the bottom of the rabbit hole. You're sure this is the key that opens the door to that wonderful place!

On the other hand, maybe if you just wish you were back . . .

The End

22   After some twisting and turning, you get the cover off the cookie jar. You are so hungry that you gobble up two big cookies before you offer one to Alice.

Alice is nibbling on hers when you notice that the house has gotten smaller. No! You are getting bigger! It must be the cookies!

Go on to the next page.

"Alice, help!" you yell, as your head pushes the roof off the house. You're so big that there's no more room for Alice in the house. She runs outside and looks at you helplessly as you grow up and up.

Oh, why did you eat those cookies? Why didn't you just TAKE ONE, as the label said.

Will you ever shrink to your proper size?

You hope you won't be quite this big when you wake up from your dream!

The End

24   You and Alice follow the overgrown path to THIS WAY. After walking a bit, you hear, "Stop!"

You look up in surprise and see a funny-looking caterpillar sitting on a mushroom.

"Why must we stop?" you ask politely. "We want to go THIS WAY."

"Well, if you want to go THIS WAY," says the Caterpillar, "you will have to go THAT WAY to get there."

Go on to the next page.

"But we don't want to go THAT WAY. That's why we picked THIS WAY!" says Alice, a little crossly.

"I just told you," says the Caterpillar, a little crossly, too. "You can't go THIS WAY *this way*."

You and Alice look at each other. You want to go THIS WAY, but you are afraid of making the Caterpillar mad—especially since he's so big!

Turn to page 26.

26   "But we don't *want* to go THAT WAY," cries
Alice. "And if we can't go THIS WAY, we can't go
anywhere!"
    "Well, that's not true at all," says the Caterpillar.
"There is always a where to go to when you can't go
where you want to."
    "Really?" you say. "Then tell us where."
    "Why you can go *nowhere*!" says the Caterpillar.
You and Alice sigh and give up.
    "There! That's settled," says the Caterpillar.

Go on to the next page.

"But don't worry," he continues. "I will entertain
you. I know all my multiplication tables and I'll
recite them for you, one after the other."

You groan and sit down. Why did you choose to
go THIS WAY? Now you're stuck with a boring
caterpillar who loves arithmetic.

What a way to spend the day. . . . What a way to
end a dream!

The End

You look high and low for the White Rabbit's gloves. In one room you find a closet with a heavy door. You go inside—and the door slams shut behind you. You try to open it but you can't. You're locked in!

"Help!" you cry, but you know that Alice can't hear you through the thick door. You will have to open it yourself.

Go on to the next page.

KEEP OUT
BY ORDER OF
TWEEDLEDUM

You and Alice continue along the path.

Soon you come upon a big sign that says KEEP OUT BY ORDER OF TWEEDLEDUM. Beyond it lies a garden.

"Who's Tweedledum?" asks Alice.

"It's such a silly name," you answer. "I'm sure it's no one important."

You want to follow a path that goes through the garden, but Alice isn't sure that's a good idea. The only other path, though, leads through some thick bushes.

If you go into the garden, turn to page 38.

If you through the bushes, turn to page 40.

"What do you mean THAT WAY leads to
THE END?" you ask the Cheshire Cat.

But instead of answering, the cat starts to
disappear!

Soon all that is left is his grin.

"Well," says Alice, "I've often seen a cat without
a grin, but a grin without a cat! It's the most
curious thing I ever saw in all my life!"

Go on to the next page.

"Me, too," you answer. "And by the way, I'm more curious than ever to find out where THAT WAY leads!"

So you and Alice continue down the path.

In a little while you come to a grove of Weeping Willow trees.

Suddenly Alice stubs her toe on a rock and starts to cry.

Turn to page 36.

You are trying to make her feel better, when a big drop of water falls on your head. Then another . . . and another and another.

Is it raining? No! It's the Weeping Willows. They are crying with Alice! They cry so hard they start a small flood!

"Stop crying, Alice," you say. "You're making the Weeping Willows cry, too!"

"I can't," sobs Alice. "It hurts too much!"

Go on to the next page.

You try to help her up, but now the flood of tears has turned into a small river. You and Alice are swept along like two leaves.

Suddenly you hear a roar. Oh, no! There's a big waterfall ahead and you are heading right for it!

"I hope this is all a dream," you say. "Otherwise going THAT WAY really is going to lead to . . .

The End

KEEP IN
BY ORDER OF
TWEEDLEDEE

You step boldly into the garden, but Alice stands back.

As soon as you enter, you feel a tug on your arm.

"I'm Tweedledum," says a roly-poly little man as he pulls you out of the garden. "Keep out!"

Then you feel a tug on your other arm.

"I'm Tweedledee, his brother," says a look-alike man, as he pulls you into the garden. "Keep in!"

Go on to the next page.

You are wondering what's going on when you see the other side of the sign, the side that's facing the garden. It says KEEP IN BY ORDER OF TWEEDLEDEE. Just then, Tweedledum and Tweedledee pull at the same time. You feel as if you're stretching.

You look at your arms—you are!

"Help!" you cry to Alice, but there's nothing she can do.

Oh, no! Now you're caught in a tug of war between two quarrelsome brothers, and you're the rope!

The End

When you come out on the other side of the thick bushes, you find yourselves in the middle of a tea party!

A funny little man in a big hat shouts, "This is the March Hare's un-birthday party. Did you bring a present?"

"Why, no," you both say.

"Good!" says the little man. "Then you're un-invited!"

Go on to the next page.

"The Mad Hatter is right," says the March Hare. "You're un-invited, so sit down!"

You and Alice sit down. In a few minutes you are caught up in the craziest party you've ever been to.

Everyone keeps switching places and switching cups, and the Hatter and Hare stuff a dormouse into the teapot!

You've never had more fun at an un-birthday party in your life!

The End

After a while you come to a clearing—and there's Alice! But she seems to be in trouble. She is surrounded by giant playing cards, and the Queen of Hearts is shouting, "Off with her head!"

You rush up to Alice and say, "Can I help?"

"Silence!" says the Queen, "or I'll have your head, too!"

Go on to the next page